tiny titans

RETURN TO THE TREEHOUSE

ROBIN, I DON'T THINK THIS IS THE RIGHT WAY TO TRAIN FOR SCUBA DIVING.

YOU'RE RIGHT! WE NEED ANOTHER PERSON!

I'M AVAILABLE.

Art Baltazar & Franco
Writers

Art Baltazar
Artist & Letterer

SUPERBOY created by Jerry Seigel
By special arrangement with the Jerry Siegel family

SUPERGIRL based on the characters created by
Jerry Siegel and Joe Shuster

SUPERMAN created by Jerry Siegel and Joe Shuster
By special arrangement with the Jerry Siegel family

TINY TITANS: RETURN TO THE TREEHOUSE

DC Comics, 2900 W. Alameda Avenue, Burbank, CA 91505
Printed by Transcontinental Interglobe Beauceville, Canada. 1/15/16. Second Printing.
ISBN: 978-1-4012-5492-6

Library of Congress Cataloging-in-Publication Data is Available.

RETURN TO THE TREEHOUSE

WE'RE BACK!
WHO'S BACK?
MY BACK!
MORE BACK THERE, TOO!

tiny titans
ROBIN
STARFIRE
RAVEN
KID FLASH
MISS MARTIAN
KID DEVIL
CASSIE
BEAST BOY
AQUALAD
WONDER GIRL
BUMBLEBEE
CYBORG
ROSE
SPEEDY

BY ART BALTAZAR & FRANCO
WRITER & ARTIST
WRITER

NOW!
LOOKING FORWARD TO SEEING THE TITANS!
CAN'T WAIT TO TELL THEM ABOUT OUR SUPER FAMILY ADVENTURES!
AND THE FORTRESS OF SOLITUDE!
RUFF!
AW YEAH!

WHAT THE--?!
THE TITANS TREEHOUSE IS... GONE!

FIVE MINUTES AGO...
titans

C'MON, TERRA!
JUST ONE PIECE!
IT'S ROCK CANDY.
YOU WON'T LIKE IT.

OH, I LOVE ROCKS!
ESPECIALLY FROM YOU!
YOU NEED TO BACK AWAY!

MAY I HAVE SOME OF YOUR ROCK CANDY? PLEEEAASSE?
ROCK CANDY

SLAM!
ROCK CANDY

YOU FORGET, BEAST BOY. TERRA CONTROLS ALL FORMS OF ROCKS.
DELICIOUS!
WEREN'T YOU TWO ALL "KISSIE KISSIE" LAST TIME I SAW YOU?

MWAH! MWAH!

CLOCK!

HE'S SO **CUTE**, ISN'T HE?
THUD!
WHATEVER.

-ROCKIN'.

MEANWHILE, OUTSIDE...
SO, WHAT'S THE FIRST BADGE REQUIREMENT?
ACCORDING TO THE BRAINIAC CLUB HANDBOOK...
...WE HAVE TO SHRINK SOMETHING.
WELL, THAT'S NO PROBLEM.
I HAVE THE BOTTLE AND YOU HAVE THE SHRINKING RAY.
OKAY, THEN...
WHAT SHOULD WE SHRINK?
HOW ABOUT THE tiny titans TREEHOUSE?
THAT'LL WORK!
titans
titans
SHRINK!

THE TREEHOUSE IS SO CUTE!
IT FITS PERFECTLY IN THE BOTTLE!

WE SHRUNK!

I THINK WE MAY HAVE SHRUNK SOME TINY TITANS IN THERE!
AND ONE OF THEM IS THROWING ROCKS!
PING
PING
PING
AWESOME!
THAT SHOULD BE WORTH AN EXTRA BADGE!

—EARN IT!

MEANWHILE, BELOW WAYNE MANOR...
...IT'S LUNCHTIME IN THE BATCAVE!
CHOMP
CHOMP
EAT
CARROT
HERE YOU GO, ACE!
SOME BAT-DOG FOOD FOR MY BAT-DOG!
WOOF.
BAT DOG FOOD
ACE
ROBIN!
SOMETHING HAPPENED TO THE TREEHOUSE!
BAT DOG FOOD
ACE

-FREAKIN' CLOWNS.

—TRANSMISSION.

SNIFF
SNIFF
SNIFF

GOOD JOB, ACE!
WOOF WOOF
RUFF
RUFF

ACCORDING TO THE BAT GPS, THERE'S DEFINITELY SOME TREE-LIKE MATERIAL IN THE SWAMP.
IT COULD BE OUR TREEHOUSE!
SNIFF
SNIFF

SUPERBOY!
GOT IT!
FEELS MOSSY.
VERY ORGANIC.

LITTLE BOY, WHY ARE YOU PULLING ON MY ARM?
I THOUGHT YOU WERE A TREEHOUSE.
DO I LOOK LIKE A TREEHOUSE?
UM... A LITTLE BIT.
SORRY, MR. SWAMPY.
SPLASH!

MINUTES LATER, ELSEWHERE...
SNIFF
SNIFF

WOOF WOOF
BARK BARK
RUFF RUFF

ARE YOU SURE, KRYPTO?
YEP. DEFINITELY SOMETHING MADE OF WOOD DOWN THERE.

GRUNDY NOT TREEHOUSE!
SORRY TO DISTURB YOUR SLUMBER, SIR.
MOVING ON!

-TREES & FIRE HYDRANTS ONLY.

LATER...
SO, THAT WAS EMBARRASSING.
WHAT SHOULD WE DO?
WE'LL NEVER FIND THE TREEHOUSE NOW!

I'LL USE MY X-RAY VISION TO FIND IT!

I SEE IT... THERE!

PSIMON AND BRAINY 5 HAVE IT!
HEY, BRAINIACS!
WHERE'RE YOU GOING WITH OUR TREEHOUSE?!
?!

WHAT TREEHOUSE?
THE ONE IN YOUR BOTTLE!

THIS ONE?
WE NEED THIS TO EARN OUR BRAINIAC CLUB SHRINKING BADGE!
IT'S OURS.
YOU NEED TO GIVE IT BACK!
NO WAY, MAN! FINDERS KEEPERS!

REALLY?! YOU'RE GOING THERE?
YEP! AND THEY ARE COMING HERE TO PICK US UP!
PICK YOU UP? WHO'S COMING?
SHAKE SHAKE
AZARATH--
WHAT'S HAPPENING?
SHAKE SHAKE
METRION--
SHAKE
SHAKE
ZINTHOS!
OH NO!

WAIT A MINUTE!
YOU COULD UNSHRINK YOURSELVES AT ANY TIME?
YEP.
THERE GO OUR BONUS BADGES!
AZARATH--
BRAINY! SHE'S TRYING TO ENLARGE THE TREEHOUSE!
RUN!

METRION--
RUN
CHASE
RUN
JOG
RUN
CHASE

RUMBLE
RUMBLE
RUMBLE

THE BRAINIAC SHIP!
AAHH!
AAHH!
WHAT THE--?! THEY'RE HERE!
LOOKS LIKE OUR BRAINIAC CLUB MEETING IS STARTING EARLY!

ZZAP!

...ZINTHOS?
OUR TREEHOUSE! BRAINIACS TOOK OUR TREEHOUSE!

MOMENTS LATER...
SAD
SAD
SAD
SAD
EXCUSE ME, MASTER ROBIN...

ALFRED!
HELLO, KIDS.
I SEE YOUR TEAM HAS LOST THEIR TREEHOUSE.
YEAH. YOU COULD SAY THAT!
THE BRAINIACS SHRUNK IT!

I HOPE YOU DON'T MIND...
I TOOK THE LIBERTY OF DESIGNING A NEW TITANS TREEHOUSE...
...WITH SOME BAT-INFLUENCE, OF COURSE.
WOW!
A BAT-TREEHOUSE!
THANKS, ALFRED!

HEY.
HOWZIT GOIN'?

ALFRED!
IT'S TOO CROWDED! THE PLACE IS FILLED WITH BATS!

OH, YOU'LL GET USED TO IT.
IT'S JUST LIKE THE BATCAVE.

MINUTES LATER...
REALLY WISH WE COULD ALL FIT IN THE NEW TREEHOUSE.
WE CAN'T EVEN GO IN.
NOT ONLY ARE THERE TONS OF BATS...

...IT'S FILLED WITH BAT-BUNNIES...

...AND PENGUINS!

—LOVE ON THE ROCKS.

POP
POP
ART
BALTAZAR
2013

tiny titans

BONUS!

BLUE BEETLE'S BACKPACK LANGUAGE TRANSLATION!

ROBIN

STARFIRE

RAVEN

MISS MARTIAN

CYBORG

BLUE BEETLE

SPEEDY

BY ART BALTAZAR & FRANCO

WRITER & ARTIST — WRITER

MEANWHILE, AT THE NORTH POLE...
HOW FAR IS IT?
ARE WE THERE YET?
JUST A LITTLE BIT FURTHER.
WHAT ARE WE DOING OUT HERE ANYWAY?
IT'S FREEZING!
WE'RE LOOKING FOR A NEW TREEHOUSE!

WHAT HAPPENED TO THE LAST ONE?
OH, YEAH.
THE WHOLE BRAINIAC SHRINKING THING.

SURE IS COLD!
I CAN'T SEE A THING!

THESE WHITEOUT CONDITIONS ARE ATROCIOUS!

I CAN'T SEE ANYBODY!
SLAP!
OW!

WOULD YOU PLEASE REMOVE YOUR HAND FROM MY FACE?

OH, SORRY.

BBZZZZ
BEEP
BEEP
RADAR
BEEP
BEEP
THAT'S IT! YOU FOUND IT!
YOU FOUND THE TREEHOUSE?
NOPE.
SHE FOUND THE FORTRESS OF SOLITUDE.
WOW! ARE WE GONNA MEET SUPERMAN?!
-START LOOKING.

WOW.
FASCINATING.

HEYA, KIDS!
COUSIN KAL!
SUPERMAN!
SO, WHAT BRINGS YOU KIDS HERE TO THE FORTRESS?

THE BRAINIACS STOLE OUR TREEHOUSE!
WHAT?!

I THOUGHT HE WAS BECOMING A GOOD GUY!
WE WERE DOING SO GOOD.

WHA--? IT'S THE SUPER HIGH-PITCH DISTRESS CALL FROM JIMMY OLSEN'S SIGNAL WATCH!
OW! TURN DOWN THE VOLUME!
IT'S SO LOUD!
HELP!
EXCUSE ME, CHILDREN...
...THIS LOOKS LIKE A JOB...
...FOR SUPERMAN!
WOW. HE'S SO COOL.
FOOSH!
YEAH. HIS SUPER HEARING IS NEVER WRONG.
I DON'T KNOW, BUDDY.
I DIDN'T HEAR A WORD YOU SAID.
THAT ZZEEE SOUND IS PIERCING!
-HUH? WHO'S CALLING ME?

WHAT ABOUT OUR TREEHOUSE?
OUR HEADQUARTERS!
RIGHT! LET'S CALL BRAINIAC!
HOW ARE WE GOING TO DO THAT WITH SUPERMAN GONE?
WE'LL CALL BRAINIAC BY USING THE KRYPTONIAN CRYSTALS!
REALLY?
YEAH! IT'S LIKE USING A SUPER CELL PHONE!
WATCH THIS!
VVZZM BEEP BEEP
BEEP BEEP
HELLO?
HI, BRAINIAC! IT'S SUPERGIRL!
WHO?
SUPERGIRL.
Y'KNOW, KAL'S COUSIN?

SIGH.

OH.
RIGHT.

VVRRMMM

SO...
... WHAT'S UP?

HAVE YOU SEEN OUR TREEHOUSE?

YOUR WHAT?
TREEHOUSE!

WHY WOULD YOU THINK I KNOW ANYTHING ABOUT THAT?
THE TITANS WERE CHASING PSIMON AND BRAINIAC 5...

... BECAUSE THEY SHRUNK THE TREEHOUSE TO GET A BRAINIAC CLUB BADGE!

THAT'S
PREPOSTER---
RIDICUL---
WE DIDN'---

PSIMON!
BRAINY 5!

YES, SIR?
DID YOU TWO
TAKE ANYTHING
FROM THESE TITANS?

NO. NOPE.
NUH-UH.
NEVER
HAD IT!

SEE, MY BOYS
DON'T LIE.
OH,
YEAH?

THEN WHAT
ARE THOSE?
THOSE ARE
BRAINIAC CLUB
SHRINKING BADGES!

OH!
I DIDN'T EVEN SEE THAT!

GOOD JOB, BOYS!
THANKS!

WELL, TITANS. TOO BAD WE COULDN'T HELP YOU.

WE HAVE TO HEAD BACK TO THE GREAT CITY OF KANDOR!

GOOD LUCK FINDING YOUR TREE.

TREEHOUSE! IT'S TREE HOUSE!

WE'RE NEVER GONNA FIND IT, ARE WE?

-HOMESICK.

MEANWHILE, OUTSIDE THE FORTRESS...
SO, WHERE'S KANDOR, ANYWAY?
I THINK IT'S IN SPACE.

IS THAT WHERE THAT THING IS FROM?
I'M NOT SURE. I NEVER SAW A SQUARE ASTEROID BEFORE.

AAWWWYEEHHGRRR!!!
TITTNNNSSS!
OH, NO.

CCSSYBR
HELLOOOO!!
IT'S MATCH!

OOF!
HHUGGZZ!

WHAT THE--?!
I HEAR YA, BACKPACK!

DEFENSIVE MANEUVER NUMBER ONE!
MISSS YUUU BOOO BEEETTLL!!
UM... HAPPY TO SEE YOU TOO, MATCH.

—EMBRACE IT!

SO, IT'S A ROCKET SHIP?
YEP, IT'S MATCH'S ROCKET SHIP.
tiny titans
HE ARRIVED HERE IN IT WHEN HE CAME FROM BIZARRO WORLD.
SO TROOO! ITZ TROO!
BIZARRO WORLD?
YEAH, THAT PLANET WHERE EVERYONE IS OPPOSITE AND WEIRD-LOOKING.
BIZARRO IS FROM THERE, TOO.
OBVIOUSLY.
SPEAKING OF...
HA! HA!
MY HOME THIS IS NEW FORTRESS HOME!
SO, MATCH IS OPPOSITE OF SUPERBOY...
AND BIZARRO OPPOSITE OF SUPERMAN...
SUPERGIRL, DO YOU HAVE AN OPPOSITE?!

–TAKE ME HOME NOW.

tiny titans
WADDLE
WADDLE
WALK
WALK

OH, HELLO.

QUACK!

I'M NOT SURE.
BUT I THINK IT'S SOME SORT OF DUCK.

DUCK ZARRO!
ME AM LOVE PET DUCKZARRO!

—READING COMICS!

OKAY, KIDS!
I HAVE A SOLUTION!
tiny titans

I CAN CREATE A FORTRESS BY USING THIS CRYSTAL!

WATCH THIS!

THROW!

BLOOP!

BUBBLE!

SPLISH!
GROW!

BEAM!

LIFT!

MOMENTS LATER...
THERE YOU GO, KIDS!
PROBLEM SOLVED!

SEE YA!
THANK YOU, SUPERMAN!

OUR NEW TREEHOUSE IS SO WONDERFUL!
YEAH! IT SURE IS GREAT AND CRYSTALLY LIKE THE FORTRESS OF SOLITUDE!

HA! THE TREEHOUSE OF SOLITUDE.

DRIP!

UM... ROBIN...
...I DON'T THINK THIS IS GONNA WORK OUT.
WHY NOT?

DRIP!

—KEEP LOOKING.

SHAZAM!
AGAIN! WITH MORE FEELING!
ART BALTAZAR 2014
I DON'T THINK THE T-SHIRT IS HELPING.
WHY NOT? IT WORKED FOR THE BUNNY!

BY ART BALTAZAR & FRANCO

WRITER & ARTIST — WRITER

tiny titans
MEANWHILE, AT THE ROCK OF ETERNITY...
I CAN'T BELIEVE YOU LIVE HERE, BILLY!

I DON'T LIVE HERE. I JUST VISIT HERE.
WHY?
IT HAS SCARY STATUES AND IT'S A BIT CREEPY.
LIKE BEING IN A CAVE.

YOU MEAN LIKE LIVING IN A BATCAVE?
UM... NOT QUITE.
BUT, WITH SOME HI-TECH GADGETS, A COOL CAR, AND SOME BATS...
...YOU MIGHT HAVE SOMETHING HERE!

ANYWAY, LET ME INTRODUCE YOU TO...THE **WIZARD**.
HELLO, SIR.

HELLO, KIDS!
WHO'S YOUR LITTLE FRIEND?
I'M **ROBIN**. FROM THE TINY TITANS.

AW YEAH TITANS!
WHOAH.

UM... NICE MEETING YOU, SIR.
LATER!

YOUR **UNCLE** IS A **WEIRD** OLD DUDE!
HE'S NOT MY UNCLE.
HOW OLD **IS** HE?
HE'S OVER 3,000 YEARS OLD.
SO, HE'S YOUR **GRANDPA**?
HE'S NOT MY GRANDPA.

HE'S AN **ANCIENT** WIZARD WHO GIVES US THE **MAGIC** TO TRANSFORM INTO SUPER HEROES LIKE...
SHAZAM!

WOW, BILLY. YOU'RE HUGE!
HEY! WHO'S THE SUPER HERO?
THAT'S BILLY.

WOW, BILLY! YOU'RE HUGE!
I JUST MET YOUR GRANDPA!
HE'S NOT MY...
C'MON!
HE SAID HE'D TAKE US FOR ICE CREAM!
HUH?

A MOMENT LATER...
OKAY, KIDS.
IF WE TIME THIS RIGHT...
...WE'LL BE ENJOYING SOME MAGICAL DESSERT IN SECONDS!

SHAZAM!
RUMBLE!

AVALANCHE

YOU'RE **RIGHT**, WIZ!
MAGICAL SNOWCONES BEAT ICE CREAM ANY DAY!
TOLD YA!
ARE YOU SURE HE'S NOT OUR GRANDPA?
I'M SURE.

–REFRESHING!

tiny titans
SO, EXPLAIN TO ME AGAIN. HOW'D YOU GET YOUR POWERS?
HOW DO THEY WORK?

I SHOUT OUT THE MAGIC WORD THE WIZARD GAVE ME...

SHAZAM!
KRAKOOM

SHAZAM!

KRAKOOM
AW YEAH!

SEE?
WOW. CAN I TRY?
SHAZAM!
HHMM... NOTHING.
OF COURSE NOT.
THE MAGIC IS A GIFT FROM THE WIZARD.

HOP
HOP
HOP

SHAZAM!
KRAKOOM
HA!

-NO PLACE LIKE HOME.

tiny titans
SO, WHATCHA DOING, TERRA?
I'M TAKING A CLOSER LOOK AT THIS ROCK OF ETERNITY.
POWERS
POWERS
POWERS

LIFT

TIP

TWIRL

STOP
TERRA!
STOP PLAYING WITH OUR ROCK OF ETERNITY!
SLAM!
THOOMP!

SORRY.

—ROCKSTAR.

tiny titans
OH MY GOSH!
I'M LATE!
LATE?
LATE FOR WHAT?
I'M GOING TO JOIN THE LEAGUE OF "JUST US COWS" TODAY!

"JUST US COWS"?
BUT YOU'RE A RABBIT!

SWOOSH!
AREN'T YOU SUPPOSED TO BE A COW?

BOY!
I CAN'T WAIT!
THIS IS GONNA BE AWESOME!

MINUTES LATER, AT THE KENT FARM...
HELLO, LADIES!
KENT

I'M SO EXCITED!
WHERE ARE THE OTHER SUPER PETS?
IT'S JUST US COWS.
WELL, I BROUGHT CARROTS!

WELCOME TO THE LEAGUE OF JUST US COWS!
YOU'RE OUR NEW MEMBER!

HERE'S THE OFFICIAL HAT!
OH, BOY! THIS IS SO COOL!

WHAT'S GOING ON IN TODAY'S MEETING?
TODAY'S A SPECIAL DAY!
YEP! YOU'RE GONNA LOVE IT!

WE HAVE A SPECIAL GUEST TODAY!
REALLY?

YEP! MAMA KENT IS COMING!
WOW!

WE'RE GETTING MILKED TODAY!
MILKED?
WHAT?

HELLO, GIRLS!

YOU'RE GONNA LOVE THIS!

WHO'S READY TO GO FIRST?
UGH...
ME!
ME!
ME!

I GOTTA GO!
SWISH!

—WITH CEREAL.

SHAZAM!

NOTHING!
I TOLD YA. THE T-SHIRT'S NOT GONNA WORK.

AW YEAH TITANS!
HI, FREDDIE.

LOOK WHAT I HAVE.
SO, WHAT YOU'RE SAYING IS...

...IF I PUT ON THIS SHIRT...

... I'M BATMAN!
DON'T BE A WISE GUY, FREDDIE.

YEAH, SILLY. YOU KNOW THE MAGIC UP HERE ON THE MOUNTAIN IS KIND OF UNPREDICTABLE.

UNPREDICTABLE? HMM...

AQUAMAN!

KRAKOW

HUH?

CATWOMAN!

KRAKOW

CLAYFACE!
KRAKOW

ETRIGAN!
KRAKOW

BIG UGLY MONSTER WITH ONE RED CLAW AND WINGS AND STUFF!
AW, MAN.
REALLY?
KRAKOW!
NNOO!!

–LATTÉ MOCHA MAGIC!

UM... GRANDPA SHAZAM... SIR?
CAN I ASK YOU FOR A FAVOR?
tiny titans

OH, THAT'S RIGHT! YOU NEED A NEW TREEHOUSE, DON'T YA?
WELL, TITANS! YOU'VE COME TO THE RIGHT PLACE!

MI ROCK OF ETERNITY ES SU ROCK OF ETERNITY!

SHAZAM!

KRAK-
OW!

WELL, HE **DID** GIVE US A NEW TREEHOUSE.

MAYBE NEXT TIME WE'LL BE MORE SPECIFIC.
WHAT ARE YOU TALKING ABOUT?
I THINK IT'S JUST FINE.
FEELING LIKE A **ROCKSTAR!**
ROCK. A BIG ROCK.
DEFINITELY A BIG ROCK.
SO CUTE.

—STONE COLD.

SO, HOW'S IT GOING DOWN THERE?
DID YOU FIND THE TREEHOUSE?
NOT YET.
BUT WE'RE MAKING GOOD PROGRESS!
ART BALTAZAR 2014

BY ART BALTAZAR & FRANCO
WRITER & ARTIST — WRITER

tiny titans
SO, WHY ARE WE DOING THIS AGAIN?

I GOT A **TIP** THAT THERE'S A NEW **TREEHOUSE** FOR US IN **ATLANTIS**!

UNDERWATER?
YEAH! **LAGOON BOY** IS GONNA SHOW ME THE WAY.
HEY, HOWZIT GOIN'?
LAGOON BOY?
YOU'RE IN A LAGOON?

—HE'S NOT CALLED "OCEAN BOY."

tiny titans
GORDON

KNOCK
KNOCK
KNOCK
GOTHAM NEWS

KNOCK
KNOCK

HI, COMMISSIONER GORDON!
IS **BARBARA** HOME?
SURE. COME IN.

HI, BARBARA!
AW YEAH TITANS!
HEY, ROBIN!
HEY, WONDER GIRL!

WHAT'S ON TODAY'S AGENDA, KIDS?

WE'RE GONNA TAKE THE BAT-SUBMARINE AND JOURNEY TO ATLANTIS!

ATLANTIS?
YEP!
THE CITY UNDER THE SEA?
YEP!

WHERE AQUAMAN LIVES?
THAT'S THE ONE.

OKAY. BEHAVE.
AND BE HOME IN TIME FOR DINNER.
THANKS, DADDY!
LOVE YOU!

WOW, BARB!
WHERE DID YOU GET A BAT-SUB?
BUMP
FROM MY DAD. HE'S REAL GOOD FRIENDS WITH BATMAN!

THAT'S AWESOME!
HEY, BARBARA! YOUR SUIT LOOKS A BIT DIFFERENT.
OH, YES!
I TWEAKED THE COLLAR AND ADDED A SKIRT!
I LIKE IT!
THANKS.
OH, AND...
YOU CAN CALL ME BATGIRL!

AW YEAH TITANS!
ARE YOU READY FOR ADVENTURE?!
I THOUGHT YOU SAID THIS WAS A SUBMARINE?
OH, IT TRANSFORMS!

WATCH THIS!
CLICK

MMMMMM

COOL!
TOLD YA!
HI, TITANS!
HELLO, BOYS!

AQUALAD AND LAGOON BOY WILL LEAD THE WAY!
C'MON! LET'S GO!
ONWARD TO ATLANTIS!

MINUTES LATER...
WOW!
IS THAT ATLANTIS?
YEP!
SURE IS!
COOL.
YOU THINK WE'LL MEET AQUAMAN?

PROBABLY.
HE'S MY UNCLE.

AAAHHH!!

THE INFAMOUS GIANT SQUID!
WHAT? WHERE?
OH, DON'T WORRY.

THAT'S TOPO!
HE'S A FRIEND.

OH, YEAH... RIGHT! TOPO IS A SUPER PET!
JUST LIKE ACE AND KRYPTO!
HE'S BIG.

C'MON!
TOPO KNOWS OF A SECRET PLACE YOU MAY ENJOY!

WHILE ON THE SURFACE...
I DON'T KNOW, MISS MARTIAN...
...DIDN'T THEY SAY WHERE THEY WERE GOING?
UNDERWATER!
OH, I GOT THAT. BUT WHERE?
IN THE OCEAN!

BUT THE OCEAN IS A BIG PLACE!
THEY COULD BE ANYWHERE!

MAYBE I CAN TAKE A LOOK AHEAD!
WHAT?!

OFFSPRING?!
HI.
WHEN DID YOU GET HERE?

OH, HEH.
I'VE BEEN HERE THE WHOLE TIME.

I'M THE BOAT.
YOU MEAN, I'VE BEEN SITTING IN YOU THE WHOLE TIME?

EEWWW!!

WHAT'S WRONG, BEAST BOY?
I SUDDENLY FEEL VERY SEA SICK.

–SEAWORTHY.

MEANWHILE,
BENEATH THE OCEAN FLOOR...
RUMBLE
RUMBLE

ALAS!
YOU FAIL AGAIN, BLACK MANTA!
CURSE YOU, AQUAMAN!
YOU CAN'T HIDE FROM THE KING OF ATLANTIS!
I JUST PUT AN END TO YOUR EVIL SCHEME!

LOOK!
IT'S AQUAMAN! KING OF THE SEA!
DEFENDER OF TRUTH!
HERO OF UNDERWATER JUSTICE!
HELLO, CHILDREN.

ARE YOU REALLY AQUALAD'S UNCLE?
YES.

I HEARD AUNTIE MERA MAKES THE BEST FISH STICKS.
OH, TOTALLY.

YOU KNOW IT!
BUMP
TRUE STORY.

I HEARD YOU HAVE AN AQUA-COW!
IS IT TRUE?
HE DOES. I SAW IT.

WELL, I DO HAVE MANY PETS...
...AND, I CAN SAY...

...I NEVER HEARD ANYTHING ABOUT...
MMOOOO!!

SWIM
SWIM
SWIM

MOO.
WELL, I GUESS...

WE HAVE AN AQUA-COW!

YYAAYY!!!

WHO WANTS DESSERT?!

YYAAYY!!!

I HOPE THEY SERVE DEVIL'S FOOD!

QUIET!
NO CAKE FOR BAD GUYS!
AW MAN!
ONWARD!
CHOCOLATE AWAITS!

tiny titans
OKAY!
LET'S TRY THIS AGAIN!

INHALE BREATH
HOLD
SPLOOSH!

HE'S THE BOAT.
I'LL NEVER GET USED TO THAT.

OH, HELLO, STRETCHY GUY.
WHICH WAY TO ATLANTIS?
KEEP GOING THAT WAY!
WHAT A NICE STRETCHY FELLOW.
HELLO, PLASTICY DUDE.

HAVE YOU BOYS SEEN THE TINY TITANS?

YEP! JUST A LITTLE FURTHER!

AIR! BLAH!

HEY! BEAST BOY!

THEY'RE OVER HERE!

AWESOME!
LET'S GET INTO CHARACTER!

SHAPE!
POP!

I CAN'T WAIT TO SEE ATLANTIS!
I HEAR THEY MAY HAVE A NEW TREEHOUSE!

WOW!
HOLY CORAL REEF, BATMAN!
GREAT IDEA, AQUALAD...
...BUT I THINK THE TREEHOUSE WOULD BE WAY BETTER IF IT WASN'T UNDERWATER.
TITANS
AND BESIDES, I HAVE TO GO.
MY DAD IS EXPECTING ME HOME FOR DINNER.
AW MAN! WE JUST GOT HERE!
-BEAUTIFUL DOWNTOWN ATLANTIS.

WELCOME TO PARADISE ISLAND!
YOU KNOW BOYS AREN'T ALLOWED TO TOUCH THE GROUND, RIGHT?
ART BALTAZAR 2014.

BY ART BALTAZAR & FRANCO

WRITER & ARTIST — WRITER

tiny titans
I'LL NEVER GET USED TO YOUR INVISIBLE JET!
IT FEELS LIKE... FLYING.
THAT'S BECAUSE WE ARE FLYING.

SEE? TOLD YA!
WONDER WOMAN...
...YOUR INVISIBLE JET IS REALLY COOL.
LOOKS LIKE WE'LL BE LANDING SHORTLY.

DO YOU BOYS HAVE YOUR SLIPPERS ON?
YES, MA'AM.
GOOD.
HERE WE GO!

THE SEARCH FOR A NEW TREEHOUSE CAN BEGIN!

I THINK WE'LL FIND SOMETHING HERE ON PARADISE ISLAND.
COUSIN DIANA HAS GREAT IDEAS!
COME WITH ME, KIDS. I KNOW JUST THE PLACE!

HEH, HEH, HEH.

AFTER WE'RE DONE HERE, WONDER WOMAN WILL NEVER FIND HER INVISIBLE JET AGAIN!

HA!
THIS CAMOUFLAGE PAINT WILL DO THE TRICK!
CAMOUFLAGE

PAINT
PAINT
PAINT
PAINT
PAINT

HEH.
HEH.
HEH.

LEAP!
LEAP!

!

MEANWHILE...
WELL, THE FIRST STEP IS TO FIND A TREE SUITABLE FOR A TREEHOUSE.

SO FAR, ALL I SEE IS PALM TREES!

IS THIS TREE EVEN STRONG ENOUGH?

KNOCK!

FALLING COCONUTS!
WATCH OUT!
I'LL CATCH 'EM!

JUGGLE JUGGLE

JUMP
BOUNCE
HOP

...AND THAT'S THE LEGEND OF THE COCONUTS OF JUSTICE!
WOW!
FASCINATING!

JUMPA!
WHAT IS IT, GIRL?!

THE INVISIBLE JET? DISAPPEARED?
WHO COULD HAVE DONE SUCH A THING?

CHEETAH AND CHAUNCEY?!

HEY, JUMPA. WHAT'S WITH ALL THE SIGN LANGUAGE?
WE SUPER PETS DON'T TALK IN FRONT OF THE HUMAN FOLK.
OH, THAT'S RIGHT!

SSHH!
WHAT?!

LET'S GO!
JUSTICE AWAITS!

WHERE'S THE INVISIBLE JET?!
I DON'T SEE IT!

IT WAS HERE!
I PARKED IT RIGHT HERE!

WE'LL HELP YOU, WONDER WOMAN!

BAM!

FOUND IT!

–HURTS.

MEANWHILE, AT SIDEKICK CITY ELEMENTARY...
SO, TELL ME AGAIN ABOUT YOUR "END OF THE WORLD" SCENARIO...
SIDEKICK CITY ELEMENTARY
SURE.
WHEN MY CUTE LITTLE BEAUTIFUL RAVEN TURNS 18 YEARS OLD...
...A PORTAL...
...GATEWAY, IF YOU WILL...
...WILL OPEN...
...AND MY DEMON FOLLOWERS SHALL TAKE OVER THE EARTH...
...WITH ME AS ABSOLUTE RULER!
SLADE OFFICE
THAT SOUNDS EXTREME!
YEAH, MAN.
IT'S GONNA BE WILD!
MAYBE YOU CAN HAVE A PRACTICE RUN ON AN ISLAND OR SOMETHING.
IT'LL BE GOOD TRAINING.
YOU KNOW, YOU'RE RIGHT!
A PRACTICE "TAKING OVER THE WORLD" PARTY!
GOOD IDEA!
WE SHOULD MAKE PANCAKES!

IT'S BEEN CAMOUFLAGED!
ONLY ONE PERSON COULD HAVE DONE THIS...
...AND MY MAGIC LASSO WILL FIND HER!
THROW!
MAGIC LASSO! FETCH ME A CHEETAH!

WHAT?
IS THAT THE MAGIC LASSO?
LOOKS LIKE IT'S BEING CONTROLLED!

I DIDN'T KNOW WONDER WOMAN COULD DO THIS!

SWIPE!

THERE'S LOTS YOU DON'T KNOW, CHEETAH!
CURSE YOU, WONDER WOMAN!

-JUSTICE!

RAVEN?
ARE YOU GETTING A TEXT MESSAGE?
YEP.
UGH.
IT'S MY DAD.

OH, NO.
HI SWEETIE!

HE'S THINKING OF HAVING A "TAKING OVER THE WORLD" PRACTICE RUN PARTY.
TRIGON?
YEAH.
COMING HERE?
YEAH.
PANCAKES?
MAYBE.

GREAT HERA!
I APOLOGIZE FOR WHAT'S ABOUT TO HAPPEN...
RUMBLE!
RUMBLE!

WOO-HOO!
HELLO, PARADISE ISLAND!
LET'S GET THIS PARTY STARTED!
NOT GOOD, DAD.

WHAT'S WRONG WITH A LITTLE PRACTICE, SWEETIE?
IT'S LIKE A FIRE DRILL!
YOU'RE EVEN IN FULL DRESS MODE!
OF COURSE!
I KNOW WE'RE SUPPOSED TO WAIT UNTIL YOU'RE 18 YEARS OLD TO TAKE OVER...
...BUT I THOUGHT A LITTLE PRACTICE MIGHT BE FUN!

KNOCK!

WAS THAT WONDER WOMAN'S INVISIBLE JET?
YES. IT SEEMS I GOT A NEW PAINT JOB.

YOU MUST WEAR THE SLIPPERS!

HOLD IT, GUYS!
STOP RIGHT THERE!
NOBODY PARTIES WITHOUT WEARING THE SLIPPERS!
AGAIN?
I HOPE THEY'RE THE PINK ONES!
THEY'RE ALWAYS THE PINK ONES.
COOL!
I BROUGHT PANCAKES!

tiny titans

HOW DO WE KNOW TRIGON IS INVADING THE RIGHT EARTH?
I HEARD THERE WERE MULTIPLE EARTHS.
HUH?
WHAT DO YOU MEAN?

LIKE DIFFERENT VERSIONS OF THE EARTH WITH DIFFERENT VERSIONS OF THE SAME PEOPLE.
THAT SOUNDS CRAZY!

SO, THERE MAY BE MULTIPLE ME'S?
IT'S POSSIBLE.

THEN THAT MEANS THERE MAY BE MULTIPLE TRIGONS, TOO!
ALSO POSSIBLE.
THAT'S RIDICULOUS!

DON'T THINK ABOUT IT TOO HARD.
YOU MIGHT HURT YOURSELF.

KNOCK!
OW!
HA! A LITTLE REMINDER FROM THE COCONUT EARTH.
GOOD ONE.

-EARTH 53.

ANYWAY...
...DID YOU EVER ASK **WONDER WOMAN** ABOUT THE NEW TREEHOUSE?
I SURE **DID!**
SHE USED HER CREATIVITY AND BUILT IT **AMAZON**-STYLE!

REALLY?
DIANA SAID IT'S VERY SIMILAR TO THE **INVISIBLE JET** TECHNOLOGY.
IT'S THIS WAY!
NEAR THE PALM TREES!

HERE IT IS!
IT LOOKS GREAT!
WHAT LOOKS GREAT?
OUR NEW TREEHOUSE!

-IT'S ALL CLEAR.

EPILOGUE:
IN THE FAR REACHES OF THE MULTIVERSE...
...FLOATS THE COCONUT EARTH...

...WHERE ITS DEFENDERS...
...THE COCONUTS OF JUSTICE...
...ARE ABOUT TO FACE THEIR BIGGEST CHALLENGE...

...THE SECRET ORANGES OF THE JUSTICE LEAGUE!

THE BATTLE BEGINS!
VS!

AAHH!!

ANOTHER NIGHTMARE?
YEP.
MONSTERS AND DEMONS AGAIN?
NOPE.

ORANGES AND COCONUTS THIS TIME.
GOODNIGHT, COUSIN.
G'NIGHT.

-VITAMIN C YA!

ART
BALTAZA
2014

BY ART BALTAZAR & FRANCO

WRITER & ARTIST — WRITER

tiny titans
SIDEKICK CITY ELEMENTARY
GOOD MORNING, STUDENTS.
WELCOME TO MATH CLASS.

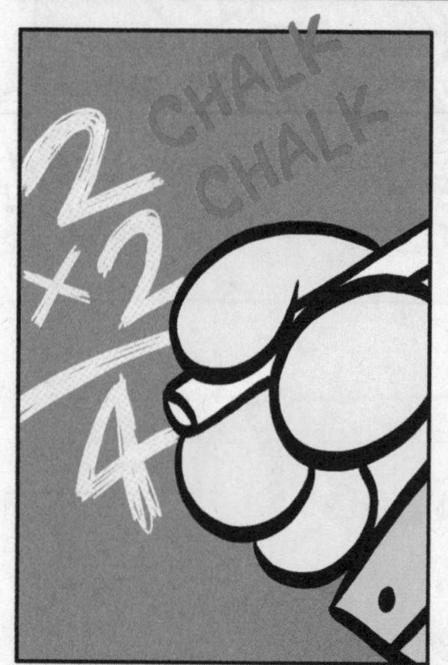
CHALK CHALK
2
x2
4

MR.
I'M YOUR TEACHER.
MR. TAWNY.

BORING. BORING. BORING.
WE SHOULD BE OUT LOOKING FOR OUR TITANS TREEHOUSE!
YEAH, THIS IS SO BORING.
HEY! I LIKE MATH.
MAYBE WE CAN CONTINUE SEARCHING AFTER SCHOOL.

PSST! TITANS!
OR MAYBE WE CAN START LOOKING NOW!
RIGHT!
CYBORG HAS SOME SWEET JUSTICE LEAGUE CONNECTIONS!

OKAY, I'M GONNA NEED A BOOM TUBE AT THE SCHOOL!
WHO ARE YOU TALKING TO?

C'MON! QUICK! LET'S GO!

HEY! STUDENTS! WHERE DO YOU THINK YOU'RE GOING?
OH, DON'T WORRY, MR. TAWNY...
...WE'LL BE RIGHT BACK!

WELL, I HOPE THEY KNOW THERE ARE NO BOOM TUBES ALLOWED IN SCHOOL!
I'LL SEE THEM IN DETENTION!
PRINCIPAL SLADE!

JLA

BOOOM!

WOW!
THE JLA WATCHTOWER!
WE'RE IN SPACE!

UM...
WE'RE IN TROUBLE!

WHO LET YOU IN HERE?

WELL, SIR...
WE HAVE THIS BOOM TUBE AND...

B'DG!

UH-OH!

YES, BATMAN?

DID YOU ACTIVATE THE BOOM TUBE?
ABSOLUTELY!

WOW!
HE TALKS!
THE LANTERN PET TALKS!

HE'S NOT A PET.
HE'S A GREEN LANTERN.

HE FILLS IN FOR HAL JORDAN AND JOHN STEWART FROM TIME TO TIME.
YEP! THAT'S ME!

AND YOU KIDS SHOULD BE IN SCHOOL.

WE'RE MISSING OUR TREEHOUSE!
I'M AWARE.

I'LL LOCATE BRAINIAC'S POSITION, THEN YOU HAVE TO LEAVE.
PING!
GOT HIM!

THIS IS A JOB FOR SUPERMAN.

CLARK!

YEAH, BRUCE?
CAN YOU CALL BRAINIAC?
SURE!

TELL BRAINIAC TO GIVE THE TREEHOUSE BACK TO THE TITANS.
YOU GOT IT!

IT'S SUPERMAN.
MMMM MMM
DON'T ANSWER IT!

BRAINIAC'S NOT ANSWERING.

B'DG.
I NEED A BOOM TUBE.

RIGHT ON!

TAP
TAP
TYPE
TYPE

BOOOM!

THROW!

BOOOM!

SWIPE!

HERE.

BUT, IT'S STILL SO TINY.

DO IT.

-LEAF ME ALONE.

BOOOM!
FALL!
OOF!
OUCH!

WOW! TALK ABOUT ROUGH LANDINGS!
I THINK WE JUST GOT DUMPED BATMAN-STYLE!
LOOK OUT!

FALL!
titans
FFBOOMSH!

WELCOME BACK, TITANS!
I SEE THE TREEHOUSE LANDED IN THE PERFECT SPOT!

-HOWDY, NEIGHBOR!

SOMEWHERE ACROSS THE UNIVERSE...
...THERE IS AN **EVIL** PLACE WITH **FIERY** PITS OF DESPAIR...

...AN AWFUL PLACE CALLED **APOKOLIPS!**

THE HOME OF THE EVIL **DARKSEID!**
ALSO KNOWN AS...

LUNCH LADY DARKSEID!!

YOU HAVE A PHONE CALL, SIR.

HELLO?

DARKSEID, OL' PAL!
HOW YA DOIN', BUDDY?
I HAVE A GIG FOR YA!

A JOB?
LUNCH LADY AGAIN?

OH.
SUBSTITUTE TEACHER?
NOW YOU'RE TALKING!
WELL... OKAY, THEN!

-SEQUEL SEQUENCING.

OKAY, KIDS.
INTO THE BOOM TUBE.
IT'S TIME FOR DETENTION.

WHAT?!
NO WAY!

LET'S GO!
YOU KNOW THE RULES.
NO BOOM TUBES IN THE CLASSROOM.
AW, MAN.

ANTI-LIFE
AB+F=
THIS IS SUCH A CRISIS.
THE **FUTURE** HAS NO **END**, MY FRIEND.

LUNCH LADY DARKSEID!

WELCOME TO YOUR PUNISHMENT.
QUIET.
TAKE YOUR SEATS...

...WHERE YOU WILL SPEND AN AGONIZING ETERNITY IN DETENTION!
WELL, AT LEAST UNTIL 4:30 PM.
SO VICIOUS!

—UNTIL NEXT TIME.